BIG BIRD'S NEW NEST

and Other Good-Night Stories

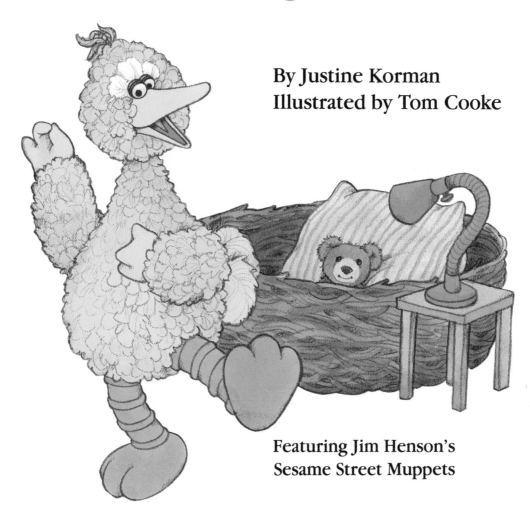

By Justine Korman
Illustrated by Tom Cooke

Featuring Jim Henson's
Sesame Street Muppets

On *Sesame Street*, Maria is performed by Sonia Manzano.

A SESAME STREET/GOLDEN PRESS BOOK
Published by Western Publishing Company, Inc., Racine, Wisconsin 53404

OSCAR'S GROUCHY VACATION

"Thank you for helping me carry my groceries," Maria told Big Bird.

"You're welcome," said Big Bird. "I like helping my friends."

"So do I," said Maria. "Please let me know if there is anything I can do for you."

"Yucch!" Oscar the Grouch grumbled in his trash can. "All this niceness is making me sick!" He banged the lid of his can, but even that dreadful din didn't cheer him up.

"I need a vacation," he said with a sigh.

So Oscar rummaged around in his can until he found a tattered flyer from Grouch Tours, Inc. It showed pictures of vacations guaranteed to satisfy even the grouchiest grouch. Oscar couldn't decide between "Town Dumps of New England" and "Trash Cans of the Rich and Famous." Then he noticed that the New England tour left in less than an hour.

"That's the tour for me," Oscar said. "I'm getting away from this sweetness now."

Oscar packed his tattered old suitcases and told the mail carrier to save all his junk mail. Then he hurried to the bus station.

"Have a nice day," the ticket-seller told Oscar.

"I hope not," grumbled the grouch. And he was so busy grouching that he forgot to find out where to wait for his bus.

Just then an announcement came over the loudspeaker: "Fall Foliage and Fun Tour departs in one minute. Grouch Tour bus leaving now!"

So Oscar ran to the nearest platform.

As soon as the bus started moving, Oscar noticed that all the other passengers were neat and cheerful. When he asked where they were going, he was told, "This is the Fall Foliage and Fun Tour."

"Oh, no! Beautiful, changing, colorful leaves? I'm on the wrong bus! Let me off!" yelled Oscar.

But the driver said, "I'm sorry, sir. The next town isn't for fifty miles."

A nice person on the bus tried to comfort Oscar.

"You'll have a fun time on this tour," he told him. "Look at that bright orange patch on the horizon! The leaves are so lovely at this time of year."

Oscar fell back in his seat, grumbling, "I might as well have stayed on Sesame Street."

The bus stopped at the side of the road, and all the passengers got off to look at the dazzling autumn leaves.

"Look at that bright yellow tree!" said a cheerful child.

"I like the red ones," another child chimed in.

Oscar didn't like the bright colors. But he did enjoy the way the leaves blew everywhere, sticking to sweaters and getting tangled in fur and piling up in messy heaps.

The next stop was the beach. Oscar ignored the glittering ocean waves and the white sand. Instead, he looked for litter and old soda bottles in the dunes.

He watched the seagulls break open mussels on the rocks, scattering shells everywhere. And he liked the seaweed the waves left behind.

When the tour stopped at a farm stand, Oscar couldn't find
anything at all to please a grouch. There were neat pyramids of
fresh apples and pears, carefully arranged jugs of apple juice, and
shelves of homemade jams, jellies, and pies. It was enough to
make a grouch scream!

Oscar took a deep breath. Suddenly he smelled something that
made his grouchy heart leap with glee.

It was the smoky smell of burning trash. Oscar followed the smell to the town dump. There he saw a group of grouches eagerly sifting and searching through heaps of abandoned bicycles, broken toasters, and beat-up egg beaters. They were looking for grouchy souvenirs.

Nearby, he saw a rusty bus with a sign that said "Grouch Tours" on the front and "Have a Grouchy Day" on the side.

"It's my group!" Oscar exclaimed, and he ran toward the other grouches. They growled glum greetings and welcomed Oscar into the Grouch Tour group.

Oscar ran from heap to heap, up to his fuzzy elbows in New England trash. Soon his fur was covered in soot.

"Now, this is my kind of vacation!" Oscar said, sighing. "Maybe tomorrow will be even worse!"

BIG BIRD'S NEW NEST

"Thanks for helping me move, Snuffy," Big Bird told his friend Mr. Snuffleupagus.

"You're welcome," replied Snuffy. "I wish I could stay and help you settle in, but we're planning a surprise party for my sister, Alice, and I need to hurry home."

Big Bird waved good-bye to Mr. Snuffleupagus and then looked around at his new home. It was full of bags, boxes, and suitcases.

"Well, I'd better start unpacking!" Big Bird said out loud.

So Big Bird moved his giant bed of twigs into a cozy corner.

"There! Now the morning sun will peep over the fence and say, 'Good morning, Big Bird. It's time to wake up.'"

Big Bird looked around. "But my new home doesn't feel like a home yet," he said.

"I know!" said Big Bird. "My new home looks like a home, but it doesn't sound like a home."

So Big Bird searched through a big box marked "records" and found his favorite, "Chirp Around the Clock." He put it on the record player and chirped and hummed along.

While Big Bird listened to the music he unpacked more boxes and bags. He moved his night table next to his bed. He found his reading lamp and put that on his night table. He tucked away his writing notebooks and a can of sharpened crayons on a little shelf over the bed.

Big Bird felt better. But somehow his new place still was not home.

So Big Bird searched through a box marked "kitchen." He found his biggest bowl, a spoon, and a measuring cup. Then he mixed a batch of his special chocolate-chip cookies. Soon his new home was filled with the warm, sweet aroma of baking cookies.

"Now my new home smells like home," he said. When the cookies were ready, Big Bird pulled them out of the oven. He bit into a warm cookie. "Now it tastes like home, but there is still something missing."

Just then a pair of round, googly eyes peeped over the fence.
"Me come in?" asked a hungry blue monster.

"Please do," said Big Bird. "Welcome to my new home. Would
you like some cookies?"

"Don't mind if I do," said Cookie Monster, and he gobbled
up all the cookies.

Big Bird smiled. "That's what my new home needed! A visit
from a friend. Now this place is home!"

GROVER, GO TO SLEEP!

Grover's mother looked at the clock and put down her book.

"It is time to go to bed, dear," she told Grover.

Grover was whirling around in his Super Grover cape and helmet, making the world safe for furry monsters.

"Do I have to?" he asked.

Grover's mother nodded. "Yes, you do."

Grover sighed. He took off his cape and helmet. He washed his
furry blue face, brushed his teeth, and put on his flannel pajamas.
But he still did not want to go to bed.

"May I please have a cup of hot cocoa?" Grover asked.

So his mommy brought him a cup of cocoa.

"Oh, my goodness!" said Grover. "You forgot the marshmallows."

So Grover's mommy went back to the kitchen and brought two marshmallows.

"Will you read me a bedtime story?" he asked.

So Grover's mommy read him a story about a prince, a princess, and a grouchy old wizard.

When it was finished, she asked, "Now will you go to sleep, please?"

"You forgot something, Mommy. You forgot to say that the prince and princess lived happily ever after."

So Grover's mommy said, "The prince and princess lived happily ever after.

"Is that better?" asked Grover's mommy.

"Yes, but you still forgot something. You forgot to say, 'The End.'"

"The End," said Grover's mommy. She smiled and kissed his forehead.

"Now go to sleep, Grover," she said.

"Okay, Mommy, but I have just one more thing to ask you. Would you sing me a lullaby?" Grover asked.

So Grover's mommy sat in her chair and rocked back and forth and sang "Rockabye Monster." She sang all the verses. She sang all the "la-la-la-las." She sang the squirrels and chipmunks on the windowsill to sleep. She sang the little bird in the tree to sleep. And, finally, she sang Grover to sleep, too.